THIS WALKER BOOK BELONGS TO:

_____

For Lalla
lots of love, Mum
V.F.

For Amelia
B.F.

First published 1995 by Walker Books Ltd
87 Vauxhall Walk, London SE11 5HJ

This edition published 1997

2 4 6 8 10 9 7 5 3 1

Text © 1995 Vivian French
Illustrations © 1995 Barbara Firth

This book has been typeset in Trump Mediaeval.

Printed in Hong Kong

British Library Cataloguing in Publication Data
A catalogue record for this book is
available from the British Library.

ISBN 0-7445-5299-0

A Song for Little Toad

written by
Vivian French

illustrated by
Barbara Firth

WALKER BOOKS
AND SUBSIDIARIES
LONDON · BOSTON · SYDNEY

Old Mother Toad
was singing to her baby:

"Croak croak croak,
Sleep, my little sweet one.
Croak croak croak,
Close your eyes and sleep."

But Little Toad didn't
want to sleep. His eyes
were bright and shining,
and he stared all around.

A sheep was standing chewing in
the field. He heard Old Mother
Toad singing, and he saw Little
Toad's bright eyes.

"Old Mother Toad," he baaed,
"Little Toad will never sleep if you
make that horrid croaking noise.
You must sing him a soft and
soothing song like this...
Baaaaa... Baaaaa...
Baaaaa..."

"Oh dear," said Old Mother
Toad, "how foolish I am."
She began to rock Little
Toad to sleep.
"Baaaaa... Baaaaa...
Baaaaa..." she sang.
Little Toad's eyes opened
wide in surprise.

A duck was swimming
up the river with her
little ones behind her.
She heard Old Mother
Toad singing, and she
saw Little Toad's
shining eyes.

"Old Mother Toad," she quacked,
"Little Toad will never sleep
if you make that silly baaing
noise. You must sing him
a cheerful song
like this..."

"Quack!
Quack!

Quackitty
quack!"

"Oh dear," said
Old Mother Toad,
"how foolish I am."

She rocked Little
Toad to and fro.

Quack!

"Quack!

quack!"

Quackitty

Little Toad sat up in his cradle and stared at his mother.

A nightingale was perched in
a tree. He heard Old Mother
Toad singing, and he saw Little
Toad's wide open eyes.
"Old Mother Toad," he sang,
"Little Toad will never sleep if you
make that dreadful quacking noise.
    You must sing him a sweet and
        gentle lullaby."
        And the nightingale
        began to sing.

He sang of the quiet velvet night,
and he sang of the glimmering
evening star. He sang of the rustle
of the tall dark reeds, and he sang
the song of the rippling river.
The sheep and the duck and
Old Mother Toad listened,
and there was a silver tear
in Mother Toad's eye.

"That was a truly
wonderful song," she
said as the nightingale
bowed and flew away.
She sighed a long sad sigh.
"I can never sing a song
as wonderful as that."
And the silver tear fell
on Little Toad's cradle.

"Mother! Mother!"
Little Toad called.
Mother Toad looked
at Little Toad lying
wide awake, his eyes
bright and shining.
"Little Toad," she
said, "when will
you ever sleep?"

Little Toad looked at his mother.
"Sing me my own song," he said.
"You have the most beautiful voice
in all the whole wide world.
Sing me my own song."

So Old Mother Toad sang:

"Croak croak croak,
Sleep, my little sweet one.
Croak croak croak,
Close your eyes and sleep."

And Little Toad closed
his eyes and slept.

MORE WALKER PAPERBACKS
For You to Enjoy

PRINCESS PRIMROSE
by Vivian French/Chris Fisher

A spoilt princess gets a lesson in having fun – and good manners – on her birthday.

"Irrepressibly witty and lively." *The Daily Telegraph*

0-7445-4315-0   £4.50

CAN'T YOU SLEEP, LITTLE BEAR?
by Martin Waddell/Barbara Firth

Winner of the Smarties Book Prize and the Kate Greenaway Medal

"The most perfect children's book ever written or illustrated…
It evaporates and dispels all fear of the dark."
Molly Keane, The Sunday Times

0-7445-1316-2   £4.99

"QUACK!" SAID THE BILLY-GOAT
by Charles Causley/Barbara Firth

The animals all go crazy, when the farmer lays an egg!

"Very attractive … very funny." *Parents*

0-7445-5246-X   £4.99

ONCE UPON A TIME
illustrated by John Prater

A little boy tells of his "dull" day, while all around a host of favourite nursery characters act out their stories.

"The pictures are excellent, the telegraphic text perfect, the idea brilliant. We have here a classic, I'm sure, with an author-reader bond as strong as *Rosie's Walk.*" *Books for Keeps*

0-7445-3690-1   £4.99